This book belongs to

_____

THE MEGASAURUS

STORY BY

Thomas Weck *and* Peter Weck

ILLUSTRATIONS BY

Len DiSalvo

LIMA BEAR PRESS, LLC
Wilmington, Delaware

Published by Lima Bear Press, LLC

Lima Bear Press, LLC
2305 MacDonough Rd., Suite 201
Wilmington, DE 19805-2620

Visit us on the web at
www.limabearpress.com

Book & Cover design by: rosa+wesley, inc.

Printed in Korea

FIRST EDITION
ISBN: 978-1-933872-12-4

Weck, Thomas L., 1942-
    The megasaurus / story by Thomas Weck and Peter Weck ; illustrations by Len DiSalvo. — 1st ed.

    p. : col. ill. ; cm. — (The lima bear stories)

    Includes learning & activity pages for use by teachers and parents.
    Summary: What's the king of Beandom to do? The tiny, multi-colored bean-shaped bears of Beandom are under attack by a monster. Even the King's wisest advisors seem unable to find a solution. Who will save Beandom? See if an ordinary, tiny bear can step forward with a plan that works.
    Interest age level: 004-008.
    ISBN: 978-1-933872-12-4

1. Monsters—Juvenile fiction. 2. Bears—Juvenile fiction. 3. Owls—Juvenile fiction. 4. Respect for persons—Juvenile fiction. 5. Monsters—Fiction. 6. Bears—Fiction. 7. Owls—Fiction. 8. Respect for persons—Fiction. I. Weck, Peter (Peter M.) II. DiSalvo, Len. III. Title.

PZ7.W432 Meg 2010

[Fic]   2009924355

K ing Limalot was in trouble. His tiny once-happy

Beandom was in trouble. In fact, all of the tiny bean-shaped

bears in his Beandom were in trouble, too. Whether they were

green like lima beans, or red like pinto beans, they were all

in terrible trouble.

There was a monster in Beandom. Tall as the tallest trees, it was so big that it made the earth tremble with each pounding step, and the trees sway when it roared. Its teeth were longer than a man's hand. It was a MEGASAURUS—and its favorite food was BEANS!

The king summoned his three wisest advisors. They were owls, of course (because everyone knows about wise old owls) and asked for their advice. The owls—named 'Howl the Owl' because he howled at night; 'Towel the Owl' as he kept a towel over one wing; and 'Vowel the Owl' because he was shaped like the letter 'O,'—looked on wisely. Howl the Owl bowed and said,

"Your majesty, we must find a different food for Megasaurus, so he will not eat beans. We will feed him pancakes."

But L. Joe Bean, a servant's son who was red like a pinto bean, shook his head. He'd heard those owls give King Limalot advice before.

"Your plan's no good. It's very bad."

Howl the owl heard him and howled;
"Silence now, you silly bean!
   You know nothing, it would seem.
   You can see my plan is good.
   It will work just as it should!"

He scoffed at L. Joe Bean. Others laughed, too. That made L. Joe Bean very sad. But King Limalot had heard what L. Joe Bean had said.

The king asked Howl the Owl, "Will you help the bakers make the pancakes?"

Howl the Owl shook with fear. "Y-y-yes, Your Majesty," he replied. After all, it was *his* idea.

The king summoned all the best bakers in the land. Great stoves were built and the bakers and Howl the Owl made pancakes as fast as they could. Soon there was a growing mountain of pancakes rising higher and higher by the hour.

Suddenly the beans felt the earth tremble and heard a terrible roar. The trees began to sway. The MEGASAURUS was coming! He sniffed the air as if to smell the pancakes. With one swoop of his mighty arm, Megasaurus picked up the pancakes and swallowed them in one gulp. Then, he scooped up Howl and all the bakers and swallowed them, too! And the rest of the beans? They scurried to hide until Megasaurus went away.

King Limalot was very scared. He quickly summoned his two remaining owls.

Towel the Owl said, "Your Majesty, we must drive Megasaurus off with bows and arrows."

L. Joe Bean shook his head.
"Your plan's no good. It's very bad."

Towel the Owl overheard him and growled:
"Silence now, you silly bean!
　　You know nothing, it would seem.
　You can see my plan is good.
　　It will work just as it should!"

He scoffed at L. Joe Bean. Others laughed, too. That made L. Joe Bean very sad. But King Limalot had heard what L. Joe Bean had said.

The king asked Towel the Owl, "Will you stand with the archers and fire upon Megasaurus?"

Towel the Owl shook with fear. "Y-y-yes, Your Majesty," he replied. After all, it was *his* idea.

The king summoned all the best archers in the land. They practiced until they could all hit the bull's eye of a target three hundred paces away—bean paces, that is.

Suddenly the beans felt the earth tremble and
heard a terrible roar. The trees began to sway. The
MEGASAURUS was coming! They fired their
arrows—so many that they darkened the sky. Their aim
was true, and every arrow hit Megasaurus. He looked
like a pin cushion, but the arrows did not harm him.

Instead, the arrows made him angry! Megasaurus blasted
such a roar it knocked over Towel the Owl and the archers.
Megasaurus fell upon them and swallowed them whole.
And the rest of the beans? They scurried to hide until
Megasaurus went away.

King Limalot was now even more very scared! He quickly summoned his last remaining owl. Vowel the Owl said: "Your Majesty, we must build a big wall around Beandom."

L. Joe Bean shook his head.

"Your plan's no good. It's very bad."

Vowel the Owl overheard him and scowled;

"Silence now, you silly bean!
   You know nothing, it would seem.
You can see my plan is good.
   It will work just as it should!"

He scoffed at L. Joe Bean. Others laughed, too. That made L. Joe Bean very sad. But King Limalot had heard what L. Joe Bean had said. The king asked Vowel the Owl, "Will you help build the wall?"

Vowel the Owl shook with fear "Y-y-yes, Your Majesty," he replied. After all, it was *his* idea.

The king summoned all the best masons in the land.
Large pebbles were gathered and the masons, along with
Vowel the Owl, built the wall.

Suddenly the beans felt the earth tremble and heard a terrible roar. The trees began to sway. The MEGASAURUS was coming! Megasaurus crashed through the wall, and the pebbles came tumbling down! He scooped up Vowel the Owl and all the masons, and swallowed them whole. And the rest of the beans? They scurried to hide until Megasaurus went away.

King Limalot was desperate and he summoned L. Joe Bean. "You seem clever," he said. "Rid this land of Megasaurus, and I will make you the Wise Bear of Beandom."

L. Joe Bean whispered a plan to the king. "Will you carry out this plan yourself?" the king asked.

"Yes, Your Majesty," L. Joe Bean said. "After all, it is *my* idea."

So the king summoned all the craftsmen and woodsmen
of the land. And at L. Joe Bean's direction, he had the
craftsmen build a giant monster mask much bigger than
Megasaurus' head and with teeth as long as a man's arm.
Next, he ordered that all the mirrors of the land be brought
to him, and he had craftsmen build a wall of mirrors wider
and taller than Megasaurus. Then he had them make a lot of
megaphones. Finally, he had the woodsmen cut one thousand
tall trees far enough through so that they were ready to fall,
and then he had each one held upright by a rope.

After everything was ready, L. Joe Bean set off to find Megasaurus. At nightfall, he found the monster. Megasaurus scooped L. Joe Bean up and was about to eat him, but L. Joe Bean called out, "Don't harm me, Megasaurus. I came to warn you of great danger."

"Great danger?" Megasaurus asked.

"Yes. There is a terrible new monster roaming the land, even bigger than you, and his favorite food is a Megasaurus."

"How can this be?" Megasaurus asked. "I am the biggest. What is this new monster called?"

L. Joe Bean thought quickly. "A-Mean-ol-Saurus," he said.

"Oh," Megasaurus said. It certainly was a scary name. He chewed his lip nervously. "I must see this A-Mean-ol-Saurus."

"Of course," L. Joe Bean said. "But the A-Mean-ol-Saurus must not see you or he will eat you up. You will have to disguise yourself. Come, I have it all planned out. I will take you to him."

It was still night-time when they got to the place where the craftsmen had built the giant monster mask.

"What a big mask!" Megasaurus said, putting it on. There were two large holes for his eyes. The top of the mask extended far above his head.

Just at daylight, they approached the wall of mirrors.

"There it is, the A-Mean-ol-Saurus," L. Joe Bean said, pointing to the wall of mirrors. You can let me off here. Walk closer for a better look. But remember, whatever you do, do *not* take off your mask or he will eat you up!"

Megasaurus set L. Joe Bean down and started toward the mirrors, unaware that all he was seeing was the reflection of himself in the super-giant mask.

Megasaurus' eyes widened at the size of the A-Mean-ol-Saurus' head. As he got closer, his eyes bulged at the sight of teeth as long as a man's arm. Megasaurus trembled at the thought of these mighty teeth eating him up.

Suddenly there was a terrible roar as thousands of beans hidden in the woods shouted all at once through their megaphones. At the same moment, the bean woodsmen cut the ropes holding up the many pre-cut trees to make them come crashing down all at once.

Megasaurus jumped with terror! He whirled about and ran as fast as he could. The mask slipped down so he could not see, and he tripped and fell with such a crash that it shook the earth and smashed the mask to pieces.

From the jolt of his fall, Howl the Owl and the bakers, Towel the Owl and the archers, and Vowel the Owl and the masons came tumbling out of Megasaurus' mouth. They were all still alive and well. Megasaurus paid them no attention. He scrambled to his feet and fled the kingdom of Beandom, never to be seen or heard from again.

King Limalot was happy. His tiny once-happy Beandom was happy once again. In fact, all of the tiny bean-shaped bears in his Beandom were happy, too. Whether they were green like lima beans, or red like pinto beans, they were very, very happy. *Except*, perhaps, for those three wise owls. They were replaced by one very wise L. Joe Bean.

THE END

EXTEND THE LEARNING

Read *The Megasaurus.*

Before reading, you might ask:

- *Describe a problem you experienced at home or at school. How did you solve the problem? Did anyone help you? Tell me how.*
- *Look at the title and cover illustration. What do you think this story might be about?*
- *Let's read* The Megasaurus *to learn about a BIG problem King Limalot needs to solve in Beandom.*

During reading, stop and ask children questions to make sure they are following along. Take time to talk about details in the illustrations to help children understand story concepts and unfamiliar vocabulary. Ask questions such as:

- *(page 3) Megasaurus was so big it made the earth tremble with each pounding step. What do you think* tremble *means?*
- *(page 7) How do the illustrations help you know why L. Joe Bean feels sad?*
- *(page 9) Who likes pancakes? How many can you eat? How many do you think the bakers made? If you put all the pancakes the bakers made into ten equal piles, how tall do you think each pile would be?*
- *(page 18) Can you fill in the missing word? "Your plan is no good. It's very _____ ."*
- *(page 27) Megasaurus puts on the giant monster mask and approaches the wall of mirrors. What do you think will happen next? Let's read to find out.*

After reading, take time to talk about the book. You might say:

- *Can you tell me what this story is about?*
- *Did the story's ending surprise you? Why or why not?*
- *How do you know L. Joe Bean is a wise bean?*
- *Let's look for interesting words in the book that describe how things move:* tremble, sway, tumbling, scurried, whirled, jolt, scrambled.
- *Can you think of another idea that might have stopped Megasaurus? What would you have done to keep Megasaurus out of the kingdom of Beandom?*

ACTIVITIES!

- **Make a Monster Mask.** Draw a mask shape on heavy cardstock. Cut out the shape, and then check that the eyeholes are in the right spot before you cut them out. Use a variety of art materials (such as colored beans, small leaves, buttons, and glitter) to decorate the mask. Tape or glue a tongue depressor, popsicle stick, or a plant stake to the back of the mask. Use the stick to hold the mask up to your face.

- **Count and Measure 300 Paces.** In the story, the best archers in the land could hit a bull's eye from 300 paces. How far is that? First, get a long piece of rope or string. Next, determine a starting point, and then start walking. Each step counts as one pace. How far do you travel in 300 paces? Use the rope to measure how far you traveled.

- **Dialogue.** Take turns role-playing the dialogue between the three wise owls and L. Joe Bean. Use different voices for each of the characters. Point to the punctuation in the dialogue: exclamation marks, commas, and periods. Talk about how these marks help readers understand how to read the story. Read the sentence before the dialogue for more information on how to read each part with meaning:
(page 7) Howl the Owl heard him and howled.
(page 13) Towel the Owl overheard him and growled.
(page 18) Vowel the Owl overheard him and scowled.

- **Word Sort.** Draw attention to the different sounds the vowel pattern *ow* makes. Write the following words from the story on separate index cards: *owl, howl, vowel, towel, now, bow, swallow, arrow, town, brown*. Slowly say each word aloud. Ask children to listen to the sound the vowel pattern makes in each word. Place words with the same vowel sound in separate piles. Then read each pile of words together.

Lima Bear and his friends go trick-or-treating on Halloween. Maskamal becomes entangled with a ghost and everyone fights frantically to rescue him only to discover that they have made a terrible mistake! What is their mistake? What can they do to show how how sorry they are for destroying the "ghost"? Read the story to find out.

THE MESSAGE OF THE STORY IS:
Make amends to those you have harmed.

$15.95

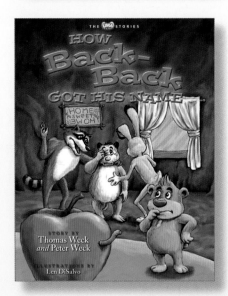

Can you imagine what it would be like to lose your back!!? Well, that is exactly what happens to Plumpton, the Opossum. Lima Bear and his clever friends become detectives searching for his missing back. Follow them as they try new and different ways of thinking to solve the mystery. See how they band together to protect each other in times of danger! Will they ever find Plumpton's back? Follow the story to find the answer.

THE MESSAGE OF THE STORY IS:
The tolerance of differences in others yields benefits.

$15.95

FORTHCOMING BOOKS BY LIMA BEAR PRESS, LLC

The Cave Monster

The Labyrinth

The Search for Back-Back's Back